DORA AND THE UNICORN KING

adapted by Ellie Seiss
based on the screenplay "King Unicornio"
written by Rosemary Contreras
illustrated by Victoria Miller

Ready-to-Read

Simon Spotlight/Nickelodeon
New York   London   Toronto   Sydney

Based on the TV series *Dora the Explorer*™ as seen on Nick Jr.™

SIMON SPOTLIGHT
An imprint of Simon & Schuster Children's Publishing Division
1230 Avenue of the Americas, New York, New York 10020

For information about special discounts for bulk purchases, please contact Simon & Schuster Special Sales at 1-866-506-1949 or business@simonandschuster.com.
Manufactured in the United States of America 0111 LAK
First Edition
2 4 6 8 10 9 7 5 3 1
ISBN 978-1-4424-1312-2

Hi! I am  !
DORA

This is !
BOOTS

Do you see a ⌒ ?
RAINBOW

Look! Someone is coming

down the .
RAINBOW

It is our friend .
UNICORNIO

Hello,  !
UNICORNIO

Do you see a  ?
DOOR

Someone is coming out

of the .
DOOR

It is a .
RABBIT

Hello, !
RABBIT

The  has a
RABBIT

message for .
UNICORNIO

The animals of the
ENCHANTED FOREST

want to be their king.
UNICORNIO

 **has to go to the**

UNICORNIO   CASTLE

to get his  **.**

CROWN

Hooray,  **!**

UNICORNIO

But is not sure

UNICORNIO

that he can be a king.

He does not think that he is

kind, smart, brave, and strong

like a king should be.

We can show

UNICORNIO

that he can be a king.

Will you help?

How do we find the 🏰? CASTLE

MAP says that we need to go

through the RIDDLE TREE.

Then we need to go

past the VOLCANO.

Then we will be at the CASTLE.

On our way to the 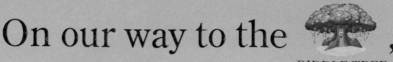 ,

RIDDLE TREE

we see a tiny 🧝.

ELF

He is too small

to reach the 🍑.

PEACHES

Who can help the 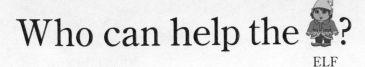?

ELF

 , yeah!

UNICORNIO

 is very kind,

UNICORNIO

just like a king should be.

We made it to the  .

RIDDLE TREE

We need to answer

the RIDDLE TREE 's riddle.

Who can answer the riddle?

, yeah!

UNICORNIO

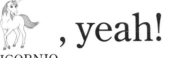 is very smart,

UNICORNIO

just like a king should be.

There is the 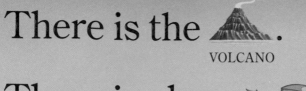.

VOLCANO

There is also a ![dragon].

DRAGON

Oh, no!

 UNICORNIO can create a  SHIELD

with his  HORN,

but we have to stomp our feet

to make a really big  SHIELD.

stomps his feet.

and I stomp our feet.

Will you stomp your feet?

Yeah! We made a big .
SHIELD

It stopped the .
DRAGON

 is very brave,
UNICORNIO

just like a king should be.

We are almost at the 🏰 .

CASTLE

Uh-oh! A 🐿 fell

SQUIRREL

into the river .

Someone needs to pull the

SQUIRREL to safety.

Who can help the ?

SQUIRREL

 , yeah!

UNICORNIO

 is very strong,

UNICORNIO

just like a king should be!

UNICORNIO is a true king!

He is kind, smart, brave, and strong.

The **RABBIT** gives **UNICORNIO** a **CROWN**.

Hooray, King **UNICORNIO**!